Tall Tales of Old India from a Very, Very, Very Long Time Ago

W9-DCE-392

LION, BULL AND TWO JACKALS
The Panchatantra Book One Retold

Narindar Uberoi Kelly

Illustrated by Meagan Jenigen

To My Love Michael J. Kelly

Order this book online at www.trafford.com
or email orders@trafford.com

Most Trafford titles are also available at major online book retailers.

© Copyright 2014 Narindar Uberoi Kelly.
All rights reserved. No part of this publication may be reproduced, stored in a retrieval system, or transmitted, in any form or by any means, electronic, mechanical, photocopying, recording, or otherwise, without the written prior permission of the author.

Printed in the United States of America.

ISBN: 978-1-4907-4028-7 (sc)
978-1-4907-4029-4 (e)

Trafford rev. 07/07/2014

 www.trafford.com

North America & international
toll-free: 1 888 232 4444 (USA & Canada)
fax: 812 355 4082

Note To The Reader

I fell in love with these stories as a tween who stumbled across them in a library at a time when my family were refugees as a result of the partition of India between what is now Pakistan and India. I suppose part of the attraction of the stories was escape from the realities of being homeless in a part of India that seemed a different country, with people speaking different languages and eating food quite unlike anything I was used to. But the stories helped me by giving me some insight into what and why my parents were trying to teach me—and some appreciation for what I was resisting in a world turned upside down by our narrow escape from the violence and turmoil of our loss of home and country.

I decided I wanted my grandchildren to have access to these stories that meant so much to me, but in a language that they could easily understand. As I adapted the stories for modern readers, it occurred to me one of the great strengths of the Panchatantra (literally the five books) derives from what at first seems the sheer nonsense of listening in to animals talking like humans. Yet this absurd conceit of animals chatting and arguing and telling stories immediately establishes a strangely safe distance between the reader and these creatures. And even more strangely, we are transformed into observers and compatriots in their struggles with thorny issues of friendship, collaboration, conflict and ambition. If I was particularly taken with these tales at a time of vulnerability and uncertainty in my life, readers approaching and experiencing adolescence and young maturity (when *does* that process end?) are in some sense similarly adrift and puzzled by the strange new land of adulthood. Readers of these tales are assumed to be much like I was--expatriates operating in a new landscape they don't fully understand.

The genius of these stories is their relentless unwillingness to whitewash or romanticize adult life. They depict the ignoble as well as the noble, cruelty and deceit as well as honor, foolishness as much as cunning, deception as rampant as honesty. They show the underside as well as glimpses of fulfillment in adult life. The stories unveil the contradictory nature of adult life, its tensions, risks and dangers as well as its rewards. And it accomplishes this through the disorienting welter of stories within stories that pile up on each other to convey a kind of confusion that forms a powerful antidote to other literary forms designed to convey wisdom—like preaching, teaching, telling people what to do. Out of this confusion, somehow wisdom can escape as a form of deeper appreciation of the perils and tensions and value of leading a good life.

Narindar Uberoi Kelly

TALL TALES OF OLD INDIA

There was a king called Immortal-Power who lived in a fabulous city which had everything. He had three sons. They were truly ignorant. The King saw that they could not figure things out and did not want to learn. They hated school. So the King asked a very wise man to wake up their brains. The wise man, a Brahmin named Sharma, took the three Princes to his home. Every day he told them stories that taught the Princes lessons on how to live intelligently. To make sure they would never forget he made them learn the stories by heart. The first set of teaching tales were:

Lion, Bull and Two Jackals

Sharma began

"The Lion and Bull
Were friends until
One Jackal intervened
Who was wily and mean
Then friendship died."

"How come?" asked the three Princes, and Sharma told this story.

LION, BULL AND TWO JACKALS

The Panchatantra Book One Retold

Narindar Uberoi Kelly

Illustrated by Meagan Jenigen

Lion, Bull and Two Jackals

Introduction

INTRODUCTION

The purpose of these stories has always been to teach basic knowledge and wisdom that makes for a better life. Each of the five 'books' in the original were organized around a theme: Loss of Friends, Making Friends, War or Peace, Loss of Gains, Ill-considered Action.

Book One, here titled simply 'Lion, Bull and Two Jackals', deals with friendship. It shows how the close friendship between the Lion and the Bull was formed, grew and eventually was destroyed by a mean and conniving Jackal. It highlights how friendship, indeed all relationships, needs tending. Cultivating friendship, like cultivating a flower, needs careful fertilizing, feeding and pruning. But the lessons go beyond how to treasure and keep enduring friendships. They include how to treat others with respect, honesty and loyalty and how to judge when others are trying to do you harm.

In the 'frame' story, Crafty, an unemployed jackal is looking to win favor with the Lion who rules his forest, introduces the Lion to the Bull. When the Lion and the Bull become close friends, Crafty seeks to destroy the friendship. Cautious, another unemployed jackal, tries to stop Crafty from doing the unforgivable. In the end Crafty succeeds and the Lion kills the Bull.

Inside the *frame* story are 33 *nesting* stories. One set (5) are stories that Crafty tells the Lion and Bull to promote himself. One set (4) are stories the Bull tells Crafty to smooth things over when his own danger becomes obvious (but he is telling them to the wrong animal). Most of the stories form the debate between the two jackals: Cautious tells stories to prevent Crafty from destroying the friendship between the Lion and the Bull (8) or Crafty tells stories to Cautious to justify his actions (7). The remaining stories are deeper *nesting stories* (9). Three stories are connected because one character appears in all of them. Two are connected because the storyteller is the same. A group of five stories illustrate a David and Goliath situation and involve ways the weak can prevail but only with the aid of friends.

Each story, or group of stories, is separated into the *frame story* of the lion, bull and two jackals, and the *stand-alone or nesting stories* that illustrate the lessons of the frame story. The frame story presents the do's and don'ts of life and is told on the left hand pages where the text is enclosed within 'a frame'. The pages on the right of the open book tell the stand-alone stories that illustrate the point or lesson articulated in the frame story. This arrangement will allow parents reading aloud to young children, or young adults, or adults of any age, to choose whether they want to read or ignore the frame stories that deal overtly with societal mores and lessons in life. The frame story on the left hand pages can be read without interruption of the illustrating stories. For the curious or the purist, the book can be read in its entirety left to right on the open pages to experience its original demanding design.

A word of caution: some of these stories illustrate Indian practices of many centuries past. Women are not often depicted or treated well, a phenomenon that continues to this day. But the stories have much to tell us. I trust that parents will help their children to understand the age-old realities described in the five books and use the occasion to teach their own values.

Lion, Bull and Two Jackals

There once was a very rich merchant who lived in a city in India called Sunrise. It was a great city: well laid out at the foot of tall mountains and very prosperous. The Merchant was content living there until it dawned on him that although he had lots of money he should try to increase it by putting it to good use. After all, riches should be hard earned, carefully protected, ever increased by savvy investing, and shared wisely. Money unused is money un-possessed.

So he collected his merchandise wagon, hired some workers, harnessed his two lucky bulls named Joyful and Lively and went forth towards a bigger city to make more money.

On the journey, the team had to go through a dense forest. When they were half-way into it, the bull named Lively snapped his yoke, fell, and badly injured a leg. Lively could not continue on the journey. So, with much regret, the Merchant ordered him to be left behind with some feed just in case the leg healed.

After a few weeks in the jungle, Lively did get better. He found plenty to eat and plenty to explore. He began to have a good time and made a lot of noise. One day a lion with a big bushy golden mane named Rusty was passing nearby with his animal staff, servants, and subjects. Rusty heard Lively bellow and was both surprised and bothered. He had never heard such a sound before.

Now a Lion, King of the jungle, has a company: the lion himself, his ministers and advisers, his attendants and guards, and his subjects, with each class divided into high, middle and low. Rusty was accepted as King by them all because of unbounded pride, exceptional courage and incomparable self-esteem that brooked no rivals. Rusty was King because he behaved like a king: fearless, valiant, dignified, ready to benefit others, without reproach, pretense and dependency. His deeds crowned him King.

Among Rusty's followers there were two jackals, sons of former ministers with some hereditary rights, but currently out of a job. Their names were Cautious and Crafty. When Crafty saw that Rusty seemed bothered by the bellows everyone had heard, he began to plot harm to Rusty. Cautious tried to stop him: "Why meddle?" he said, "remember the wedge-pulling monkey." "Come again?" asked Crafty. So Cautious told this story.

Wedge-Pulling Monkey

A wealthy merchant was having a temple built. Every afternoon the workers would take a break and go have lunch away from the site. One day, a troop of monkeys from a nearby park came by and began climbing all over the unfinished temple. It was such fun. One of them noticed a wedge put up by the workmen at the very top of the building frame to keep a huge log from rolling down. Without a thought the curious monkey pulled the wedge to see what would happen. Well, the big log rolled down and crushed him before he could get out of the way.

"That is why bright people avoid meddling" said Cautious. "We may not be employed by King Rusty but we pick up enough to make do even as hangers on." Crafty wasn't having it. "We could be hired if we show good service and someone else could be fired if not deserving." "What are you implying?" asked Cautious. "King Rusty is scared and his servants are scared and don't know what to do." said Crafty. "How do you know?" asked Cautious and Crafty replied *"intelligent men can infer correctly from other people's body language what is going on.* I am a judge of occasion and know how to follow dos and don'ts like:

Look for the right time to try persuading someone;	*Be cautious;*
Don't take what belongs to others;	*Stay close to those in power;*
Love the King's friends and hate his foes;	*Serve only masters who have merit;*
Invest only where there is profit;	*Always be ready to flatter;*
Above all, get to know your King.	

So Crafty went to meet Rusty and said "I know you do not need me right now but I want to see if I can be of use to a master who is fair in his dealings. After all, the quality of the servant depends upon the use the master makes. I am only a jackal but my worth is not in my birth but deeds."

"Speak freely" said Rusty.

"Why did you turn back when you heard a bellow?"
Rusty pondered: even Kings find comfort in sharing their troubles with honest and faithful friends and servants. He seems trustworthy. I will tell him.

"Some monstrous creature has come to my jungle. He is unknown but his bellow must match his nature and power. He sounds dangerous, so I turned back" replied Rusty.

"What!" Crafty said. "Frightened by a sound? The wise do not leave without making sure that the new place will be better than the old. Besides, there are many sounds that do not warn of danger. Remember how easily one can be fooled. Remember the jackal and the war-drum." "How so?" asked Rusty, and Crafty told this story.

Jackal and the War-Drum

A hungry jackal was searching for food to eat. He came upon a king's battleground in the middle of a forest and suddenly heard a loud sound. He did not know the sound and got really scared, thinking: What kind of creature made that sound? It must be huge. I am dead.

But keeping his wits he started to cautiously, quietly, look around and saw a war-drum. He did not know what it was. He noticed the sound came from it but only when a tree branch hit it when the gust of wind happened. The jackal got less and less scared and more and more curious. Maybe I can eat this creature and satisfy my hunger. It is fat. But the jackal was very surprised when he tried to take a mouthful. "What a fool I am" laughed the jackal. "I thought it full of fat so I crept in to find nothing but old wood and dry skin.

"However," objected Rusty "my servants are too frightened to go explore the sound". "I will go see" said Crafty. "Be brave until I return."

When Crafty left, Rusty began to have second thoughts. I was too trusting to show fear to this jackal. *I should have remembered that the careful, even when weak will be enemy safe, while the too trusting strong will fall quickly to the foe.*

Meanwhile Crafty had discovered the bull named Lively and gleefully started plotting to get Rusty into his power by suggesting war and peace with Lively.

Crafty went back to Rusty. "Did you see the creature?" asked Rusty. "Yes" said Crafty "and with your permission, will bring him to you." Crafty then went to Lively. "Our master, Rusty, wants to know why you are not afraid to do all this bellowing." "Who is Rusty?" asked Lively. "What!" said Crafty "you do not even know our master Rusty? He is a mighty lion, king of the jungle, with lots of ministers, servants and subjects, the proud lord of life and riches." When Lively heard this he thought: I am dead. In despair, he asked for help from Crafty. "You seem nice, please ask your master to give me safe passage and I will leave." "You stay right here" said Crafty. "When I have an agreement from Rusty, I will come and take you to him."

Crafty went back to Rusty and said "This creature has the blessings of the Great God Shiva to make this forest his playground." "What did you say to him?" asked Rusty. "I said this forest is the domain of Rusty, the mount of Great God Shiva's wife. So you are a guest. Come meet Rusty and make your home with him: eat, drink, work, and play with him." "As long as you make your master grant me safe passage" stressed Lively. "That's up to the master" said Crafty.

"I will grant him safe conduct but Lively must take an oath to me" said Rusty.

Crafty thought: the master is gracious to me and ready to do what I say. So he went to Lively, gave the bull the good news, but also made him promise to always act in agreement with him, who would play the role of counselor from now on. With such an alliance both Crafty and Lively would enjoy King Rusty's favor. "Remember, Lively, to always pay honor to a King's people" said Crafty. "How come?" asked Lively, and Crafty told this story.

Merchant Able

There lived a merchant named Able who did all the city business where he lived and all the royal business. People were satisfied. He was very clever to be able to do this for it is hard to serve two masters, city and the king, when things that have to be done are often contradictory.

When Able's daughter was to be married, the Merchant invited all the citizens and all in the king's company, paid them much honor, feasted them, and gave them presents. When the wedding was over, he escorted the King and his ladies back to the palace all the while showing great respect.

Now, the King had a house-cleaner named Bull who had once taken a seat that did not belong to him in the presence of dignitaries and Able had cuffed him and shown him the door. Bull had felt so humiliated that he could not get over it. But while the old insult still rankled, he also knew he could do nothing.

Until one day he was sweeping near where the King lay half-awake in his bed, he saw a chance to get even, so he said out loud "How awful it is, Able kissing the Queen!" The King jumped up and wanted to know if Bull spoke the truth. "I had a bad night, your majesty, and do not remember what I said." replied Bull. But the King was jealous and suspicious remembering all the proverbs about unfaithful women. He promptly withdrew his favor from Able who was very shocked for he had never done any unfriendly act against the King or anyone else.

One day, after some time had gone by, Bull disrespected Able in public and finally, Able put it all together. *He realized that servants like Bull get just as upset as anyone else when shown public disrespect.* Clearly Bull had nursed the old grudge and when he got a chance at payback, he took it. Able decided to make amends. He gave Bull a big present and explained that Bull had made a social mistake for which he had been cuffed and humiliated. Bull was thrilled with the present and apology and promised to make things right with the King.

The next day Bull entered the palace and again went near to where the King was half-sleeping and said in a loud voice: "Gee! When the King is on the toilet, he eats cucumbers." "What!" shouted the King "How dare you!" "Oh King, I had a bad night and know not what I say" answered Bull. The King realized that Bull's earlier comment about Able must have been untrue also and gave the Merchant his honors back.

*

Lively got the point of the story and agreed to the respectful alliance that Crafty wanted. Together they went to Rusty's camp and Crafty introduced Lively who bowed low to the King. Rusty extended his paw and was respectful in return.

Rusty asked Lively why he lived in the forest and Lively told him how he came there. Rusty promised to allow Lively to live his own life in the forest and even suggested Lively stay nearby so Rusty could offer protection from the other savage creatures.

Time went by and Rusty and Lively became good friends. Since Lively had lived with people and was well educated, he taught Rusty judgment. He weaned Rusty from forest habits and gave him village manners. They were together all the time and kept others at a distance. Even the two jackals, Cautious and Crafty, could not get easy entrance. Worse, because they could not share in the bounty of the lion's hunts, all of Rusty's animal followers were going hungry.

Now we all know that servants leave when they see no reward and stay if there is pay. All creatures live off each other. Kings live off countries; doctors live off patients; merchants off customers; the learned off fools; clergy off couples; thieves off the careless; flirts off lovers; and workers off everyone. Creatures set traps, wait night and day and, when given a chance, pounce like big fish on small fish.

Cautious and Crafty, robbed of their master's favor, hungry, tried to figure out what they should do. Cautious thought: *Even when masters won't take advice, good counselors should warn the King.* "Besides" he told Crafty "you are the one who introduced Lively to Rusty." "You are right" agreed Crafty. "Think of the jackal at the ram fight or what happened when Cheat played tricks, or even the meddling friend." "How so?" asked Cautious, and Crafty told these **three** stories one after another.

Pious and Cheat

A holy man named Pious lived in a secluded monastery. He performed sacrifices for people who in turn gave him beautifully woven fabrics. He sold the fabric and made a large sum of money. Once rich, he came to trust no man. He always kept his treasure beside him for he knew that money is hard to get and keeping it is harder still. Now

a con man named Cheat noticed Pious' treasure always under his arm. How can I get the treasure, Cheat asked himself? He decided to win Pious' confidence by becoming his disciple. He vowed to be clever in his flattery. "O holy Sir" he said bowing low to Pious. "All life is vanity. Can you help teach me how to escape?" Pious was impressed and replied respectfully "My son, you are blessed to realize this when so young. Deep prayer is the way." Cheat fell to Pious' feet and asked Pious to impose a vow of poverty on him. Pious complied but told Cheat to never enter Pious' cell at night. He knew that *much is lost through careless action.* So Pious told Cheat to sleep in a hut of thatch at the monastery gate.

Cheat became Pious' disciple but Pious still kept his treasure under his arm. Cheat thought: May be I will have to kill him to get the treasure. But then, as chance would have it, the son of an old friend of Pious came and invited Pious to his house for a baptism. On the way to the friend's house they had to cross a river so Pious carefully wrapped his treasure in an old robe, prayed, and gave it to Cheat for safekeeping. The minute he had the parcel in his hands, Cheat took off with it.

Jackal At The Ram Fight

Continuing on his journey, Pious was taking a break, resting peacefully, when he saw a herd of rams, and two were fighting. They butted heads and horns and there was blood. A jackal stood between the rams lapping up the blood. Well, well! Thought Pious, what a stupid jackal! If that jackal stays where he is and happens to be between the rams when the fight begins again, he will certainly be killed. The greedy jackal did not move away, was caught between the crashing heads and was killed. Feeling sorry for the jackal, Pious returned to the river to get his treasure.

When he failed to find Cheat or his treasure, although his old robe lay where he had given it to Cheat, Pious fainted. When he came to, he started shouting "Cheat, Cheat! Where did you go after robbing me?" and he started to track Cheat down.

*

The Weaver's Wife

As he was looking for Cheat, Pious met a Weaver who along with his wife was on his way to a nearby city to buy liquor. Pious begged the Weaver for some food and shelter. He reminded the Weaver that charity to the poor wins favor in God's eyes. Hearing the request, the Weaver told his wife "Go with our guest. Treat him well and respectfully. Give him food and shelter. I will go on alone to the city and return with meat and wine" and took off. The wife turned back home with Pious and was happy to do so for she was already thinking of another man. She gave Pious a broken down cot and said "Holy Sir, my girlfriend has come from the village and I must speak to her. I will be back shortly." She put on her best clothes and left to meet her lover.

Just then she ran smack into her husband who had returned reeling drunk. She ran quickly back to the house and got quickly into her ordinary clothes. But the Weaver had seen her and noticed her finery. Previously he had heard gossip about her so now his anger flared and he shouted "You slut! Where were you going?" "I have been here since I left you" she replied "You are a drunkard and make things up." But the Weaver got even madder at her lies, beat her limp with a rod, tied her to a post, and fell into a drunken sleep. At this moment, finding that the Weaver was asleep, the Barber's wife, the go-between friend of the Weaver's wife, came in and said: "Hurry up! Your lover is waiting for you." But the Weaver's wife said "I cannot possibly go right now." "For a woman of spirit" said the Barber's wife "this is no way to behave to a lover. The Weaver is helpless in a drunken sleep and will not wake until the morning. I will set you free and take your place. But hurry back."

Meanwhile, Pious who lay awake, had witnessed the whole matter. Presently, the Weaver's wife came home and found to her horror that her husband had mistakenly cut off the nose of the Barber's wife thinking it was she. She freed her friend, took her position, and shouted "Oh you stupid fool! I am a true wife. You cannot disfigure me. May the Gods make my nose whole and if I ever had any desire for other men, may they reduce me to ashes." The Weaver looked at his wife's nose and was amazed. He freed his wife and tried hard to win her back. Pious had seen the whole business and was also amazed. Heavens! Pious thought to himself, women are very clever even as they are very wicked, all poison within and all honey without. At the same time, the go-between Barber's wife with her nose cut off wondered what she could do to hide her loss. Her husband who had spent the night as required in the King's palace came home and said "Bring me my razor-case. People in town need my services and I have to clean up." His wife had a sudden idea and gave the Barber a single razor. The Barber got angry for he needed the whole case, so he flung the single razor at his wife. Immediately she seized her opportunity and ran from the house screaming "I am a faithful wife. But look! My husband cut off my nose. Help! Help!" The police arrived, flogged the Barber, tied him up and took him to court with his nose-less wife. The Jury men asked the Barber why he had done such a terrible thing, but he was so amazed at his plight that he said nothing. The jurymen took his silence as a sign of guilt. For them the guilty person is afraid but the innocent is indignant. They pronounced: "The legal penalty for assaulting a woman is death." But Pious intervened. He went to the officers of justice and said "You are making a big mistake. Please listen to me." And he told all three stories. The Barber was freed, his wife punished by having her ears cut off as well, and Pious returned to the monastery muttering to himself "The jackal at the ram fight, I, tricked of my treasure, and the nosy friend, we all three cooked our own goose!"

Having heard Crafty's stories Cautious asked "What are we to do?" Crafty was ready with an answer. "Our master has fallen into serious vice." "What are you talking about?" inquired Cautious. Crafty proceeded to count the seven, truly grave, vices, or as some say, types of evil:

Drinking,
Womanizing,
Hunting,
Gambling,
Verbal Abuse,
Greed
and Cruelty. The first four arise from unbridled passion, the last three from unbridled anger.

"Together," Crafty explained, "*they form a single vice, that of Addiction. But, really, there are five vicious situations: Deficiency, Corruption, Addiction, Disaster and Bad Policy.*

Deficiency is lack of king, minister, subjects, fortress, treasury, punitive authority, allies.
Corruption is when subjects, individually or collectively, start breaking laws.

Addiction is divided into love-group (drink, women, hunting, gambling) and anger-group (unwarranted blame of innocents, unjust taking of another's property, and unreasonable, ruthless punishment).

Disaster is act of God, fire, flood, famine, disease, plague, mass panic, hurricane.

Bad Policy is mistaken use of the six strategies: Peace, Alliance, Entrenchment, Invasion, War, Duplicity.

"Our master Rusty has fallen into the very first vice, that of Deficiency. He is so taken by Lively that he pays not the smallest attention to counselors or any of the other six supports of his throne. He must be detached from Lively. No lamp, no light." said Crafty. "And how will you do that?" objected Cautious. "You have no power!" "My dear fellow, I am thinking of how the crow-hen killed the black snake" replied Crafty, and told this story.

Crow-Hen and the Black Snake

Once, a Crow and his wife built their nest in a huge banyan tree. Every time the Crow-Hen had chicks, a great black snake would crawl up the hollow trunk of the tree and eat the chicks. But the poor crows would not leave. You know what they say: the deer, the coward, the crow cannot be induced to go when things go wrong but the lion, hero and elephant always do.

Eventually, the Crow-Hen begged her husband "I cannot stand it any longer. There is no love like the love of children and we will never have any in this deadly place. Let us make our nest in some other tree." The Crow was very depressed but answered "We have lived in this tree for a long time and cannot desert it. I will try to figure out some way to kill our enemy." "But this is a very poisonous snake. How can you kill him?" asked the wife. "I know I do not have the power myself" replied the Crow. "Still, I have learned friends and I will go ask their advice." So he flew to another tree under which lived a jackal who was a friend and told his painful tale. "Please, can you advise?" he asked the Jackal. "The killing of our children is sheer death to my wife and me." "Do not worry" said the Jackal "the heartless cruelty of the vicious black snake will itself bring his end. Remember what happened to the greedy heron." "How so?" asked the Crow, and the Jackal told this story.

Heron That Liked Crab-Meat

There was once a Heron who lived near a pond. He was getting very old and tried to find an easy way to catch fish. He began to loiter at the very edge of his pond pretending to be muddled and not eating even the fish well within reach. In the same pond lived a Crab. One day the Crab asked "Why don't you eat and have fun catching fish?" The heron answered "There soon will be a great disaster which will befall the pond, so I am depressed." "What kind of disaster?" asked the Crab. "Today I eavesdropped on fishermen who are planning to come tomorrow or the day after with their fishing nets to catch fish here." When the pond creatures heard this, they all feared for their lives and begged the Heron to save them. "I am a bird and cannot fight men. But I can transfer some of you from this pond to another, a bottomless one where you would be safe." The pond creatures were led astray by the speech and each shouted "Me first! Take me first."

Then the old crook did what the fish begged, he picked some up in his bill, carried them quite a distance to a big flat rock and ate them there. Day after day, he made the trip and had a feast while keeping the trust of the pond creatures.

One day, the Crab, who was afraid of death if left behind, begged the Heron to take him also. The Heron, bored with eating fish, readily agreed to take him next. He picked up the Crab and flew away. When he was going to land on the usual rock ledge, the Crab asked "Sir, where is the pond without any bottom?" The Heron laughed. "See that rock? That is where all the fish found peace and now it is your turn." Oh dear, thought the Crab, *friends or enemies, everyone serves their own ends. One should shun false and foolish friends.* The Heron is clever but he picked me up. Now it is my turn to catch his neck with all claws before he lands and drops me. When the Crab did so, the Heron tried to escape but had his head cut off.

The Crab painfully made his way back to the pond dragging the Heron's neck. "Why did you come back?" asked the remaining pond creatures and he told them how the Heron had fooled and betrayed them all. "I have brought back the Heron's neck to show you he is dead. Forget your worries. All creatures can now live in the pond quite safely."

*

"But how will the vicious snake meet his end" asked the Crow. The Jackal advised: "Go to some King's favorite spot. Seize a gold chain or necklace from any rich man who is careless. Then put it somewhere that when found by the guards, the snake will be seen and killed."

So the Crow and Crow-Hen flew away. The Crow-Hen was first to reach a pond where the King's ladies were bathing having left their jewelry on the bank for safekeeping. Quickly she seized a gold chain and flew back to her tree. The King's servants had seen the theft, picked up clubs, and ran in pursuit. Meanwhile the Crow-Hen quickly dropped the golden chain in the snake's hole and watched from a distance. When the King's men found the hole and the gold chain in it they saw the black snake. They killed the snake and recovered the chain. Since then, the Crow and his wife have lived in peace and happily raised a large family in their life-long home.

So the saying goes: "*Where brute force cannot work, a shrewd device may. Some heedless men may allow a petty foe to grow beyond control but for the intelligent, there is nothing they cannot control. Intelligence is power.* Where power joins with folly the rabbit lives and the lion dies." "How so?" asked Cautious, and Crafty told this story.

Arrogant and the Rabbit

There was a lion named Arrogant who was so full of himself that he killed every animal he saw just because he could. All the other forest animals – deer, boars, buffaloes, wild oxen, rabbits – got together and in despair begged Arrogant "Please, O King, Stop your meaningless slaughter. The Holy Book says that sins in this life will have to be paid for in the life hereafter. Only fools pave the way to Hell. Please stop killing everyone and if you will but stay home, we ourselves will bring you one animal each day for food." The animals went on to remind Arrogant that:
The King who does not overtax his subjects rules longest.

The King who tends his subjects is the only one who can become rich.

Arrogant was convinced and agreed that he would stop the killing only if one animal came to him every day. So each day at noon, one animal appeared as his dinner. Each species took its turn and provided a willing animal, grown old, or religious, or grief-stricken, or fearful of the loss of son or wife, and ready to make a sacrifice.

On rabbit-day, the animals gave directions to a rabbit to go to the lion's den. The Rabbit thought to himself I wish I could kill this lion but how can I? I am just a rabbit. But then he thought with wisdom and resolution and flattery, surely all enterprise will succeed. I can kill even a lion! So the Rabbit started very slowly, knowing he would be late, all the way trying to figure out a way to kill the lion. Very late in the day he appeared before the lion who was very hungry and very angry. The lion was thinking I must start killing animals first thing in the morning! The Rabbit approached slowly and bowed slowly. The Lion saw that the Rabbit was not only late but was really too small for a meal and blew up: "You rascal. First you are too small for a meal. Second, you are late. Because of this wickedness, I am going to kill you and tomorrow I will go back to killing every animal I see whether I am hungry or not."

The Rabbit bowed lower and said "Master, the fault is not mine nor of the other animals. Please listen to the cause!" "OK, Hurry up. What do you have to say?" said Arrogant. "All the animals recognized today that it was rabbit-day and because I am quite small, they sent me with five other rabbits. But in mid-journey there sprang from a great hole in the ground another lion who asked: Where are you going? I explained that we were sent as the dinner for Lion Arrogant according to our agreement. Is that so? He said. This forest belongs to me! All forest animals, without exception, must bow to me. Arrogant is a thief. Bring him here at once and whichever of us proves stronger will be King of all animals in this forest. I" said the Rabbit "am here at his order."

"So take me to this upstart lion." said Arrogant. "Where there is no prospect of a great and sure reward and the risk is great and sure instead, he should not have picked a fight!" "But, Master, he came out of a fortress and *an enemy in a fortress is hard to beat*" remarked the rabbit to which Arrogant replied "Show me the imposter even if he is sneaking in a fortress. I will kill him. For *the strongest man who fails to crush at birth disease or foe, will later be destroyed by that which he permits to grow.*" "Follow me, Master" and the Rabbit took Arrogant to a well where he said to the lion "Master, who can endure your Majesty? The moment he saw you, the thief crawled into his hole. Come, I will show him to you." The Rabbit showed him the well where Arrogant, big fool he, seeing his own reflection, hearing the echo of his own roar much magnified, hurled himself into the well, falling to his death. The Rabbit, in high spirits, returned to the other animals, gave them the good news, accepted their compliments, and lived to be a very old rabbit.

"But that is a special case. Even if the Rabbit was successful, *the weak should not deal fraudulently with the strong*" objected Cautious. "*Weak or strong, one must make up one's mind to vigorous action*" retorted Crafty. "*Unceasing effort, not fate, brings success,*. In fact, the very gods befriend those who always strive and not even Brahma sees through well-devised deceit. Remember the weaver who was persistent and won the Princess." "How was that?" asked Cautious, and Crafty told this story.

The Weaver Who Loved A Princess

The Weaver and the Chariot-Maker were good friends. They lived and worked in Sugarcane City. They were master craftsmen who earned enough to be not bothered about keeping financial accounts. They wore high-end high-fashion clothes, were always well-groomed and moved freely in high society.

One day there was a big city festival and everyone put on their best and went to the fair. So did the Weaver and the Chariot-Maker. As they wandered looking at people and things, they got a glimpse of Princess Lovely who was seated at the window of the King's handsome stone palace surrounded by girlfriends. She was drop-dead gorgeous, with a beautiful body and an unusually lovely face. The Weaver was stricken by Cupid's arrow and could not see anything but the princess and her beauty. When he got back home, he lay in bed reciting poems that might be able to express his love.

When the Chariot-Maker arrived the next morning, he saw the unkempt love-sick Weaver and quickly diagnosed the problem. "The King belongs to the warrior caste while you are a tradesman. Have you no respect for the Holy law?" he warned. "But" the Weaver replied "the Holy law also allows a warrior three wives. Perhaps one wife of the King may be a woman of my caste, which would justify my love for her daughter, the Princess Lovely." Seeing his friend in such an awful state, the Chariot- Maker relented and told the Weaver that he would try and figure out a way by which the Weaver could win his lady.

The following morning, true to his word, the Chariot-Maker brought with him a brand new mechanical bird, which looked like Garuda, the golden eagle of God Vishnu, but made of wood, brightly painted, with all kinds of neat plugs and levers. "My bird" he told the Weaver "will take you where you want to go: push in that plug to start and pull it out to stop. Tonight, when the world sleeps, dress up like Vishnu, mount this Garuda-like bird, and fly to the palace to meet your Princess who sleeps alone on the palace balcony." So, just past midnight, the Weaver followed his friend's instructions. The Princess was thrilled to be chosen as the love object of God Vishnu. She did not know, of course, that her lover was a Weaver dressed as Vishnu who proceeded to tell her that she was really his wife fallen to earth by a curse and that he had come to wed her by the marriage ceremony used in heaven. So she married him that night and they made love every night from then on. Vishnu would leave in the morning. Eventually, the guards in the women's quarters realized that the Princess was spending the nights with a man and in fear of their lives reported to the King. "O King, we beg personal safety for we need to tell you a secret." The King agreed and the guards told him that Princess Lovely was meeting a man every night. "What do you want us to do?"

The King was troubled and contemplated how from the time a daughter is born to him, a father worries about picking the right husband for her. It sure is difficult to be the father of a girl! Whenever a poem, or daughter, is born, the creator is filled with doubt: *Will she reach the right hands? Will she please as she stands? And what will the critics say?*

The King went to the Queen for advice. She went to their daughter "You are a wicked girl! You have brought disgrace to this royal family! Tell me the truth!" And the Princess told the story of the Weaver disguised as Vishnu. The Queen was delighted believing that the God Vishnu had married her daughter in a ceremony used in heaven. She hurried to tell the King and they happily decided to hide that night and witness Vishnu's coming.

When they realized that their daughter had truthfully described Vishnu's visits, the King said to the Queen "You and I are truly blessed to have the God Vishnu in love with our daughter. Now, through the power of our son-in-law, I shall be able to rule the whole world."

At this time, representatives came to collect the annual tribute due Emperor Valor, who was lord of the whole South, all nine million nine hundred thousand villages. But the King, full of his newfound relationship with Vishnu, did not treat them with the customary humility and respect.

The representatives got angry: "Pay up, King. Have you become Superman with special powers that you can afford to irritate Emperor Valor, himself a death-God?" The King actually mooned them and they returned to their country exaggerating their insult a thousand fold and making their master very angry indeed.

Emperor Valor got his troops together and marched northward to wage war against the King of Sugarcane City. He arrived uninterrupted and destroyed everything in sight as he went through the country. But the King was not concerned. His people saw that they were surrounded by Emperor Valor's troops and begged their King to do something. "Why are you so unconcerned?" they asked and the King replied "Wait until the morning."

Meanwhile, he sent for Princess Lovely and affectionately approached her "Dear daughter, we are relying on your husband's power in the hostilities we have begun against the enemy. Please ask blessed Vishnu to kill our enemy". When Vishnu came that night, Lovely passed on the King's request. The Weaver laughed and said "Tell the King not to worry. In the morning Vishnu will kill your enemies with his discus."

The King was overjoyed when he heard what Vishnu had said and made a proclamation to his people: "Whatever you grab from the battlefield tomorrow will remain your personal property." The people were delighted and sang the King's praises.

Meanwhile, the Weaver was debating with himself: If I fly off on my machine, I will never see my love again and her parents will be killed by Emperor Valor. If I do battle, I will meet death and with it my love will die. Either way, I will die – of lost love or lost battle. Besides, it is possible that Emperor Valor's army will be fooled and thinking me Vishnu, will flee.

When the Weaver decided upon battle, the real Garuda reported to the real God Vishnu about the imposter in Sugarcane City and said "If the Weaver dies in battle, there will be a scandal. Men will say that God Vishnu was slain by a man. People will lose faith and offerings will diminish. Atheists will destroy temples. What do you want to do?" "You make a good case" said Vishnu "Perhaps we had better lend the Weaver our powers to slay King Valor."

When the battle began and the Weaver-Vishnu swooped down on the mechanical bird-Garuda everyone was amazed. Even the other Gods came to look. Even the great God Brahma was deceived. King Valor was slain and all earthly kings came to beg Vishnu for mercy. Vishnu proclaimed "Your persons are secure from now on if you obey the commands of the local king." From then on the Weaver enjoyed all the advantages of being Princess Lovely's earthly husband.

Having heard the whole story, Cautious understood that Crafty was resolved to proceed against Lion King Rusty and gave his blessing.

Crafty went to see King Rusty. "Where have you been?" asked Rusty. "O King, there is urgent business for you. I have unwelcome news which I would much rather not have brought, but *devoted servants need to speak the unpleasant truth to their masters.*" "What are you talking about?" asked Rusty. "Lively, whom you have trusted, has been heard to speak treason. Now that he knows you so well, He plans to kill you and seize the royal power for himself. I am here to warn your Majesty who is my hereditary lord and master."

Rusty was thunderstruck and devastated. Crafty, correctly judging his state, went on: "No King should ever delegate to one individual all the powers of state, for eventually such a person will want to become King himself." "Lively is my servant. Why should he have a change of heart toward me?" asked Rusty. "Once dear is always dear." "For that very reason" went on Crafty "*there is a serious flaw in the business of getting on in the world. Everyone, of high birth or low, when given a chance will aspire to seize the throne.* Your good feelings for Lively are misplaced. *Never leave tried and loyal servants and counselors for someone new and unknown,* as Lively was to you." "But" interrupted Rusty "broken promises are a shame and I promised Lively safe-conduct." "Remember, my Lord, *caress a rascal as you will, he was and is a rascal still; you cannot straighten a mongrel's tail. You must always listen to sound advice no matter who gives it.* Remember the story of the ungrateful man." "Which one is that?" asked Rusty, and Crafty told the following story:

Grateful Animals and Ungrateful Man

There once was a poor Brahmin named Sacrifice. Every day his wife would nag: "Mr. Lay About, your children are starving and you do nothing but hang around. Go somewhere, no matter where, get some food and hurry back."

So one day Sacrifice went off on a long journey which took him through a deep forest. While wandering in it, hungry and thirsty, he came upon an old well, pretty much hidden by grass growing around it. When he looked down into the well, he saw a tiger, a monkey, a snake and a man at the very bottom. Of course, they also saw him.

The Tiger shouted: "Noble Sir, there is great merit in saving someone's life. Will you please pull me out so that I may live with my wife, sons, relatives and friends." "But I am scared of you." To which the Tiger replied *"Forgiveness is granted even to the killer, the treasonous drunk, the lying sinner, but there is none ever given to the ingrate.* I promise by a triple oath that you will never be in any danger from me. Have pity and pull me out." The Brahmin thought even if disaster results from saving a life, the disaster leads to salvation, and he pulled the Tiger out.

Next, the Monkey asked "Holy Sir, pull me out too" and the Brahmin pulled him out too. Then the Snake said "What about me, pull me out too." But the Brahmin answered "I tremble at the mere sound of your hiss, how much more at your touch!." "But", said the Snake, "we are not free agents. We bite only under orders. I bind myself by a triple oath that you need have no fear of me." The Brahmin pulled him out too. Then the animals advised the Brahmin "that man down there is a bad, bad, man. Do not trust him. Do not pull him out."

The Tiger then invited the Brahmin to his home on the north slope of a nearby mountain so he could return the Brahmin's kindness. And the Monkey invited him to his home beside the waterfall. And the Snake reminded the Brahmin "In any emergency, remember me" and all three went away. Meanwhile, the man kept shouting from the bottom of the well "Brahmin, pull me out too." In the end, the Brahmin took pity and thinking he is a man like me, pulled him out too. The man said "I am a goldsmith and live nearby. If you have any gold to be worked into shape, bring it to me and I will get you a good price" and started for home.

Sacrifice continued his journey but found nothing whatever. Dejected, he started for home but remembered the Monkey. So he paid a visit, found the monkey at home, and received delicious fruits that revived him. Besides which the Monkey assured him that if he ever needed fruit, he should come to him any time.

The Brahmin then went to visit the Tiger who surprised him with a gift of a gold necklace he had taken off a prince he had killed the day before. The Brahmin took it readily, thinking he would go to the Goldsmith who would do him the favor of getting it sold for him. After dinner, the Goldsmith asked the Brahmin "how may I help you?" and the Brahmin gave him the necklace which the Goldsmith recognized as the one he had made for the prince the year before. Asking the Brahmin to wait in his house, he took it to the King. On seeing it the King concluded that the Brahmin had killed his son, and ordered the Brahmin be captured and hanged the next day.

When the Brahmin was caught, he realized I did not do what the tiger, the monkey and snake advised and so that dreadful ungrateful man has brought me down. He also remembered the Snake who, as promised, appeared at once and asked "How can I serve you?" "Free me from these fetters" begged the Brahmin. "I will bite the King's dear Queen and set it so she will recover only by your touch. Then you will go free." This, the Snake did.

Once freed, the King asked the Brahmin "How did you get the gold necklace?" The Brahmin told him the whole story. When the King understood the facts, he arrested the goldsmith and gave the Brahmin a thousand villages and made him a privy counselor. Sacrifice, however, gathered his family, relations, and friends around him. He wisely took delight in everyday living, while acquiring great merit by performing many services to others thus also gaining great authority by careful attention to all phases of royal duty.

Having told the story, Crafty continued "My Lord and King, you associate with Lively, making a very serious mistake that results in neglect of *the three things worth living for: virtue, money and love.* Despite my protests, my Lord and King goes his willful way, ignoring my advice. In the future, when the crash comes, do not blame the servant."

"So, should I not warn him?" asked the Lion. "Oh, No" replied Crafty. *"It is only wise to warn an enemy by action not word."* "After all" said Rusty "he is a grass nibbler. I am a carnivore. How can Lively hurt me?" "That's just the point" said Crafty. Even the weak but malicious fool can hurt you in unexpected ways. Lively, living beside you, is always spreading his dung far and wide. In it the worms will breed. The worms will find cracks in your battle-scars and will bore deep. As the proverb says *"With no stranger share your house*: Leap, the flea, killed Creep, the louse."

"How so?" asked Rusty, and Crafty told him this story.

Leap and Creep

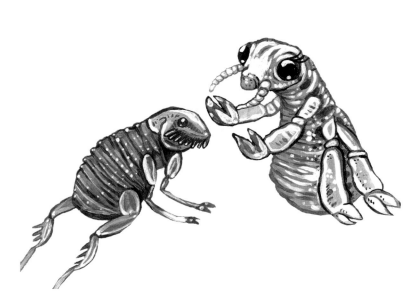

In the palace of a famous King there was a magnificent bed with all kinds of comforts. And in a corner of the quilted bedspread there lived a female louse called Creep. Every night, surrounded by a very large family of children and grandchildren, she drank the King's blood as he slept. On such a healthy diet she had grown plump and very attractive.

One day a flea named Leap drifted in on the breeze through the open window of the King's bedroom and landed on the bed. Leap was delighted with the luxurious bed and hopped around happily testing its qualities until he suddenly met Creep. "Where did you come from?" shouted Creep. This is the King's bed. Be gone at once." "Lady" responded Leap, "you should remember that I am a guest, even if unexpected, and the whole world treats guests with due hospitality and respect. I have figured out that this is a rich and healthy man's bed. Therefore, with your permission, I will sample his rich and healthy blood combining pleasure and gain." "No", said Creep, "you don't know your position and like a fool forgetting duty, time and place, you will fall by the wayside." But Leap fell to his knees and again beseeched Creep's favor. She, remembering that *spurning a suppliant enemy was always a mistake*, finally gave in. But she did caution Leap, "Do not feed at the wrong time and the wrong place." "What is the wrong time and the wrong place", asked Leap, "I have no idea." "When the King's body is overcome by drink, tiredness, or deep sleep, then one may quietly bite him on the feet. That is the right time and the right place." But Leap did not bother to follow the advice. He was hungry and the King had just gotten into bed when he bit him in the lower back. As if stung by a hornet, the King jumped up and shouted to his servants. "Something bit me! Hunt through this bed until you find the culprit and kill it." Leap quickly hid in a crevice in the bed so when the servants searched the bedding they found only Creep and her family which they killed right away.

"And that is why I say" said Crafty "*never share your home with a stranger.*" In addition, my Lord and King, you do wrong in neglecting the servants who are yours by inheritance. Remember *whoever leaves his friends to cultivate strangers will ultimately perish like Fierce-Howl.*"
"How so?" asked Rusty, and Crafty told this story.

Blue Jackal

A jackal named Fierce-Howl lived in a cave just outside a fairly big city. One day he went hunting for food. He was starving, his throat hurt, and he wandered into the city after dark. Right away the city dogs surrounded him, snapped at his heels with their sharp-pointed teeth and terrified him with their menacing bark. Trying to escape, he ran this way and that, until he reached the home of a dyer. He rushed to hide in the dyer's work area and accidentally fell into an indigo vat. Seeing him fall in, the dogs went home.

However, Fierce-Howl's time was not yet up. Eventually, the Jackal managed to climb out of the vat of indigo dye and escaped into a forest. There, all the nearby forest animals who caught a glimpse of him, dyed as he was a bright indigo blue, cried out in awe "What animal is this with such an extraordinary color?" Their eyes reflected their terror and they shouted out this news through the whole forest. "We are going to disappear. For the proverb says: *When you do not know stock, character, or strength of a possible enemy, it is best not to rely on luck.*" Now, Fierce-Howl understood their dismay and called out "Why do you flee in terror? God Indra knowing that you have no ruler right now has chosen me to be your King. Rest assured and come live safely with me."

Hearing this, the lions, tigers, leopards, monkeys, rabbits, gazelles, jackals and all other forest wild-life humbly bowed to Fierce-Howl and asked "Master, tell us our duties." Thereupon, he appointed the lion prime minister and the tiger lord of the bedchamber, while he made the leopard the custodian of the King's snuff box, the elephant the doorkeeper, and the monkey the bearer of the royal parasol. But to all the jackals, his own kind, he ordered a flogging and immediate exile. Then Fierce-Howl went about enjoying a king's glory, while the lions and others killed food animals and laid them before him. These he divided and distributed to all, after the manner of Kings.

Time passed pleasantly. One day, he was sitting in court when he heard the beloved loud sound made by a pack of jackals who were howling nearby in unison. Hearing it, his skin tingled, his eyes filled with tears of joy, and in kinship he leapt to his feet and began to howl in a piercing tone. When the lions and all other animals heard him, they realized that he was a jackal. They stood around for a minute, shame-faced and downcast, then said to themselves "Look, we have been deceived by this jackal. Let the fellow be killed." When Fierce-Howl heard this verdict, he tried to flee but was torn to bits by a tiger and died.

Then Rusty asked Crafty "How will I know that Lively is treacherous and wishes me harm? What is his fighting technique?" Crafty answered readily. "Normally, he comes into your presence with limbs quite relaxed. If, today, he approaches timidly, but obviously on the ready to pierce with his horns, then the King will know that he has treachery on his heart." Crafty then left to go visit the bull.

Crafty showed himself sluggish and dejected to Lively. Lively noticed and asked "My friend, are you in good spirits?" To which Crafty replied "How can a dependent be in good spirits? *A never-ending train of sorrows follows those in service of a king. There are five types of people who live death-in-life: poor man, sick man, the exile, the fool, and the servant of a king. The servant lives a dog's life but dogs can do things they like, a slave must obey his king.*" Listening to this, Lively figured Crafty had a hidden purpose in mind, so he asked "Tell me what is bothering you." Crafty replied "Well, you are my friend, I cannot help telling you what is in your best interest. Rusty is mad at you. He said today "I will kill Lively and invite all who eat meat to a feast. Of course, on hearing such words I fell into deep despair. Now you must do what this crisis warrants." Lively was thunderstruck and also fell into a deep depression. As he grew more and more troubled, he became panic stricken and said "If one has given cause for enmity, one may recover by removing it but how can one placate anger of a mind that is filled with hate without any cause? What wrong have I ever done our Master Rusty?" "Friend," said Crafty "Kings injure without cause and are always looking for the most vulnerable spot of any possible opponent." "True, very true" said Lively. I should have known *no blessing comes without some pain.* The fault is mine. *I chose a false friend. Harsh talk, untimely action, false friends should not be ignored.* Think of the swan sleeping among the lilies who was killed by the arrow." "How was that?" asked Crafty, and Lively told him this story.

Swan and Owl

A Swan lived along the edge of a fairly big lake. He led a good life with many pastimes. One day he had a visit from Owl. Surprised, the Swan asked Owl "Where are you from and why are you here?" The Owl replied "I have heard about your many famous virtues." The Swan was flattered and readily invited the Owl to stay with him for as long as he wished. So the Swan and the Owl from then on lived pleasantly together for many years.

However, one day, the Owl announced that he was going back home and added that if the Swan ever wanted to visit him, he would be most welcome.

Many years passed, the Swan grew old, and eventually decided that a change would be good for him. So he went to visit the Owl. He found the Owl not only much older but living in an ugly hole and quite blind in the daytime. "My dear Owl, remember me? I am your old friend, the Swan, come for a visit." The Owl answered "I don't go out in the day but we can meet at sunset." The Swan had to wait a long time and after a brief chat, he fell asleep quite near the Owl's nest hole.

As it happened, a contractor and his crew were spending the night nearby. The contractor rose early and blew the whistle to depart the campsite. The Owl immediately responded with a loud piercing hoot and then dived back into his hole. The contractor, taking the hoot as an evil omen, ordered a crew member, an archer who could take aim by sound, to shoot his sharp arrow in the Owl's direction. The arrow, alas, pierced the sleeping Swan and he died.

After telling the story, Lively went on: "King Rusty was all honey in the beginning but now he is full of poison. I sure have learned a lesson about *false friends who deceive with warm praise in your face and harsh criticism behind your back.* I am a vegetarian bull, how can I have a true friend who eats meat? Wise men rightly say: *When two are of equal wealth and status, marriage and friendship thrives, but not between rich and poor.* I have entered the false friend's lair and will forfeit my life. I should have remembered how Ugly's trust was abused." "How was that?" asked Crafty, and Lively told this story.

Gullible Camel

There was once a merchant who loaded valuable fabrics on the back of a hundred camels and set out to trade. As they were crossing a forest, one of his camels, named Ugly, hurt his ankle and had to be left behind. Poor Ugly limped around in pain, ate what grass he could find, and before long got some of his strength back and went deeper into the forest.

There lived a lion named Haughty, who had three dependents: a leopard, a jackal and a crow. They followed him around and survived on his left overs for food. Haughty had never seen a camel and asked the Crow to find out what had brought the exotic creature to his forest. When the Crow did so, Haughty felt sorry for Ugly and promised him safe conduct.

One day Haughty was himself badly injured in a fight with an elephant whose tusk had pierced his side, which meant he could not kill the food animals that he and his followers lived on. So he told the others "You will have to fend for yourselves. But if you kill a big animal, I will help you cut it up so all of us can share it." So the four animals went in search for a suitable food animal. When they did not find any, they thought of killing Ugly. "But", said the Crow, "the Master promised the Camel his personal safety." "So he did" answered the Jackal. "I will go talk to him." When he found Haughty, he said to him "We are starving and too tired to keep going on with the search for a food animal. You also need food. What do you say to eating Ugly's flesh?" "How dare you!" said Haughty, "I promised him safe conduct, the most valuable of life's gifts." "Yes, Master, I understand your situation. But no blame will attach to you if Ugly volunteers to die for your well-being. Otherwise, you will have to eat one of us, your faithful servants who have been with you for a long time." "Very well," said Haughty, "you may do what you want."

The Jackal returned to the others and convinced them that as loyal servants their only option was to offer themselves as food to their Master. First, the Crow offered himself: "Pray eat me and prolong your life at least for a day." The Jackal quickly objected "But your body is too small" and went on to offer himself. "Please Master, use my body to lengthen your life and thus make my sacrifice my ticket to heaven." At which the Leopard interrupted: "Your body is also not big enough. Master, make way for me and my loyalty and grant me glory on earth as well as an everlasting home in heaven." Hearing this, poor simple Ugly thought to himself well, they may have used fancy words to volunteer to die, but the Master did not kill a single one of them. So I will do the same and, no doubt, all three will contradict me. So he said to the Leopard "Now it is my turn" and turned to Haughty. "Master, you surely should not eat them. Pray prolong your life with mine and give me the honor and rewards of the sacrifice." At which point, the lion gave the order. The Leopard and Jackal tore the body, the Crow the eyes, and every one feasted on poor gullible Ugly.

After telling the story to Crafty, Lively went on brooding. "But *a king with false advisers is no good for his dependents in the long run. It is better to have a vulture as a king advised by swans, than a swan as king advised by vultures who always counsel evil that ruins the king in the end.* Remember the lion and the carpenter." "Why?" asked Crafty and Lively told another story.

Lion and Carpenter

There lived a Carpenter who liked to break for lunch and went every day to a nearby forest with his wife to eat and fell some trees for his wood. They each enjoyed their time together. One day, a lion named Spotless came upon the Carpenter and his wife. The quick thinking Carpenter, seeing the lion, decided it was probably wiser to face the lion than flee. So he bowed low to the lion and said "Welcome friend. Please join us for lunch. My wife has cooked a delicious meal." The lion considered the respectful invitation and graciously replied: "Although I am a meat-eater, I will be polite and have a taste. What kind of dainty snacks do you have to offer?" So the Carpenter gave him all the choice pieces of his own lunch. Spotless enjoyed the novelties and promised the Carpenter and his wife safe conduct through his forest. For which the Carpenter invited the lion to come and have lunch with him every day. "But, please come alone." In this way Spotless and the Carpenter spent their lunch time every day in good fellowship. However, the lion's followers, the Jackal and the Crow, who lived off the lion's leavings were going hungry so they approached the lion. "Please, Master, where do you go every lunch time? How come you return looking pleased?" Spotless readily told them about his new found friend the Carpenter with whom he ate a delicious lunch made by the Carpenter's wife. The Jackal and Crow immediately began plotting to kill the Carpenter because he would be good food that would last them a long time. But Spotless overheard and scolded them. "How can you think of such treachery? You know I promised the Carpenter his safety. However, if you like you can accompany me next time and I will get a delicious morsel for you also."

So the three set off at lunch time the next day to find the Carpenter. While they were still far away, the Carpenter saw them coming and he and his wife quickly climbed up a tall tree. The lion came near and shouted "Why are you up in the tree. I am your friend Spotless." The Carpenter stayed in the tree. "Your Jackal is not trustworthy and the Crow has a sharp beak. I do not like your friends!"

"So," said Lively, "*a king with false advisers can bring harm to his dependents*." And he continued to think aloud "What should I do? I suppose I must prepare to do battle." When Crafty heard this, he thought Lively has sharp horns and is very strong. He could actually strike down the Master. Then, what would happen to me? I had better dissuade Lively from fighting. So he said to Lively "Don't be hasty. *Without first finding out an enemy's strength you could lose.* Remember the sand-piper bested the sea." "How come?" asked Lively, and Crafty told this story.

Sand Piper and The Sea

A sand piper named Brag and wife called Steady lived by the sea. The sea was full of water creatures: small fish, big fish, all kinds of shell fish including oysters, and even seals and sharks. When it was time for Steady to lay her eggs, she asked Brag to please find her a safe spot. "Why?" asked Brag. This little inlet has been our home for ages. Lay your eggs here." "No way" she responded. "Right there is the mighty sea. He might send a high tide one day and wash away my newborn babies." But Brag continued to argue "The Sea knows me. Surely the mighty sea will not show enmity towards me! How could he be so foolish?"

Steady, however, laughed saying "Stop boasting. *How can you fail to judge your own strength and weakness? Although it is hard to know one-self, accurate self-assessment keeps the wise safe in times of danger. It is best to take advice from those who are your true friends.* Remember the foolish turtle who lost his hold on the stick and died?" "How did that happen?" asked Brag, and Steady told this story.

Turtle and the Two Ganders

A turtle named Shell-Back and his two friends, ganders, called Skinny and Stocky, lived in a small lake surrounded by low hills. One year, as they were faced with a twelve-year drought, the two ganders began to worry. "This lake will go dry. We need to find another body of water. But first, let us say goodbye properly to our dear old friend, Shell-Back. When they called on the turtle and told him they were thinking of leaving, he objected strongly "I am a water-dweller. When the lake goes dry I will perish from loss of water and friends. Please rescue me. The drought just means no ready food for you but it means no life for me. Loss of life is far more important than loss of good ready food." "How can we help you?" asked Skinny and Stocky. "You are a water-creature without wings and we travel by flying." Shell-Back however had an idea, "Bring a stick of wood" he requested. When they did, he explained his thinking. I will grip the middle of the stick with my teeth. You two take hold of each end with your beaks and you fly through the sky until you see another lake with water that you like." "But" the ganders warned "you will not be able to say a word on the journey or you will fall to your death!" "Not to worry", said the turtle, I will promise to be silent." So the three friends started on their journey. As they flew over a nearby city, the people below shouted to each other "What on earth are the geese carrying?" On hearing the shouts below, the turtle mistakenly asked his friends "What are the people shouting about?" The minute he opened his mouth, the foolish turtle fell to his death and the city people enjoyed his meat.

*

Having told the story of Shell-Back, Steady added *"forethought and ready wit always win out and the fatalist always loses."* "How so?" asked Bragg and Steady told the story of the three fish.

Forethought, Ready Wit and Fatalist

There were three full-grown fish named Forethought, Ready Wit, and Fatalist who were close friends and lived in a big pond. One day, Forethought was swimming close to the bank where some fishermen were standing talking. Since they were obvious enemies, Forethought decided to eavesdrop. "Lots of fish in this pond, so tomorrow we will fish here." "Oh dear," said Forethought to himself "These fishermen will soon be here. I will have to take Ready Wit and Fatalist away from here to another lake." So he went to his friends and told them what he thought. Immediately Ready Wit said "I have lived here a long time and like this lake. I do not want to move. So I had better figure out a way to protect myself from the fishermen." But Fatalist simply said "perhaps the fishermen won't come here. There are other lakes they can fish in. Besides, one should not keep making plans, for quite often they turn out to be quite unnecessary. I am going to do nothing". When Forethought understood that his friends' minds were made up, he swam upstream from his lake to another pond all by himself.

The next day, the fishermen showed up with nets and caught many fish including Ready Wit and Fatalist. Ready Wit, while still in the water played dead and so when the fisherman checked the nets they quickly threw the dead- seeming fish back into the water for they only wanted fresh fish. Of course, they killed and prepared Fatalist for their dinner.

*

But the sand-piper, Brag, was still adamant. "Why do you think me like Fatalist? I can and will protect you. Don't worry." So Steady gave in and laid her eggs by the small inlet. In time they hatched safely. But the mighty Sea had been listening all this time to the sand-piper couple. "This Brag really is very conceited. Let me put his strength to the test."

So when Brag and Steady left to go hunt for their food, the Sea made a higher than usual tide and took away their chicks. When they returned and Steady found the nest empty, she was distraught. "See, I told you so! The sea has taken my eggs. I told you more than once. Now I am so miserable that I shall die." "Please", said Brag "wait until you see what I can do. I will dry up that villain sea with my bill." "How can you? It will be impossible!" replied Steady. Still Brag insisted "*Success depends on iron-strong will-power*, nothing else." Finally Steady gave in saying "O.K. But at least call on other birds for help before you begin this enormous task. *For there is always strength in large numbers.* Even the sparrow, with help from the woodpecker, gnat and frog, brought down the elephant." "How?" asked Brag, and Steady told this story.

Sparrow versus Elephant

A Sparrow and his wife lived in a thick forest and had their nest pretty high up in a maple tree. That is where the Sparrow-Hen laid her eggs. One day in the late spring an elephant who was bothered by the heat took shelter under the same tree. He was blinded by sweat and without thinking pulled at the main branch with his long trunk, broke it, and brought down the nest. The eggs were smashed but the Sparrows themselves had a narrow escape.

The Sparrow-Hen was devastated at the loss of her chicks and could not stop crying. A Woodpecker friend of hers came over and tried to console her with this advice: "My dear friend, why cry in vain? As the saying goes *the only difference between the wise and the foolish is that the wise do not cry for what is past, dead or lost.*" "That is a good practice," said the Sparrow-Hen "but it was the elephant who carelessly killed my chicks. Why don't you think of a way to kill him? It would lessen my sorrow to see him pay for what he did." The Woodpecker knew that *a friend in need is a friend indeed, for when you do not need anything everyone is your friend.* So she must somehow help her friend the Sparrow-Hen. "Let me see what I can do" said the Woodpecker. I will go see my friend the Gnat and bring her back to figure out together how to kill the elephant."

When the Gnat understood the problem she said "There is only one way to proceed. I have a very good friend, a Frog. Let us go ask his advice for plans devised together by true friends usually work out well." So all three went to the Frog and told him the whole story. "One creature, even if it is an elephant, is weak compared to the combined strength of many. You, Gnat, must go buzz enticingly in the elephant's ears so that he will close his eyes. Then you, Woodpecker, will peck out his eyes. After that, I will trick him into thinking that there is water nearby which might give him relief. Instead, I will lead him to the edge of a deep pit I know where he will fall in and die."

"That is exactly how the three friends killed the elephant" said Steady to Brag.

*

Hearing this story, the Sand-Piper agreed. "All right. All right! I will assemble my friends and together we will dry up the sea." At which time, Brag called on each and every bird he knew and told them how the sea had destroyed his chicks. As they all started to beat their wings to bring some relief to Steady, one bird said " It will be hard to dry the sea by beating our wings. Why don't we fill up the sea with clods of clay and gravel instead." Then another bird said "Why don't we ask the advice of the wise Old Gander who lives near the big banyan tree. *You know they say it was old timers with long experience who gave the wise advice that freed the wild-goose flock held captive.*" "How was that?" asked the birds, and the old bird told this story.

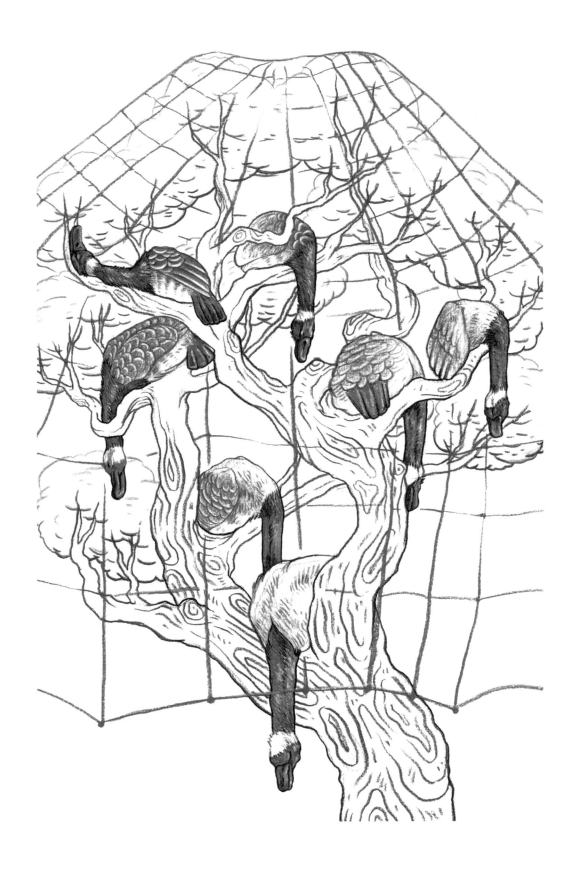

Clever Old Gander

There was a big fig tree that stood in the middle of the forest and had many broad branches. In this tree lived a flock of wild geese. In time, there grew a vicious creeping vine underneath it. Noticing it, the Old Gander said "This vine that is beginning its climb up our fig tree bodes ill. Someone could easily climb up it one day and kill us. We should cut it down while it is still thin and easily cut." But the geese disliked his advice and decided to do nothing. The vine eventually wound around the tree all the way up the trunk of the fig tree.

One day, when the geese were away searching for food, a hunter came by, easily climbed up with the help of the vine, laid a trap and went home for the night. When the geese returned they all got caught in the net. "Oh dear, the very disaster I predicted has come true and we are all caught and in danger of dying" thought the Old Gander. The geese, realizing their mistake, begged him to let bygones be bygones. "Please Sir, help us now. What should we do now?" The Old Gander replied "If you are really ready to take my advice, play dead when the villainous hunter returns. Thinking us dead, he will simply throw each of us to the ground and not first bind us. When the last one is on the ground, and he is still up in the tree, we must all rise up in unison and together fly away as fast as we can."

Early the next morning the hunter arrived and saw the "dead" flock of geese and threw them down one by one. The geese followed the advice of the clever Old Gander, waited for the last goose to hit the ground, and then flew away together.

*

When the story was finished, all the birds decided to go visit the Old Gander themselves. They told him how sad and upset they were about the taking of Steady's chicks. He responded with "Our King is Garuda. So we need to arouse his feelings with a loud chorus of weeping and wailing so that he really knows our sorrow and feels with us. When he does that, he will remove our pain." So all the birds went to find Garuda, Bird-King.

As it happened, Garuda was on his way to meet his master, God Vishnu, to prepare for a mighty battle between Gods and Demons. The birds petitioned Garuda for help, pointing out that they were weak and one of their own had been badly treated by his servant, the Sea. "Divine Garuda" they requested "please help us. The chicks were stolen when the Sand-Pipers were getting their food. As you know, *the poor must feed in secret, out of sight.* After all, we cannot do so in plain sight. Remember the Ram was killed by the Lion for doing so." "Remind me." said Garuda, and an old bird told this story.

Lion and the Ram

There was once a Ram who got separated from his flock and roamed alone in the woods. He looked very strong with his thick fleece and big horns, so most animals left him alone and he was quite content being by himself.

One day, a Lion with a large retinue, saw him looking very confident and powerful, and was somewhat scared because he had never before seen a ram in his woods. So much so, that the Lion thought to leave the Ram alone and backed away from confrontation.

Later that same day, however, the Lion saw the same Ram quietly grazing among the trees. "What! The creature is a grass-eater and as his strength can only depend on his diet, he cannot be very powerful." So the Lion quickly attacked and killed the Ram.

*

Just then, God Vishnu's messenger arrived and relayed an order to go at once to the divine city. Garuda replied "What will the Master do with such a poor servant as me?" "Better come. No need to show your pride even if you don't like God Vishnu's order." said the messenger. "But" insisted Garuda, "the Sea, the resting place of God Vishnu himself, has stolen the Sand-Pipers' chicks and the birds are my servants. Tell God Vishnu that if I don't scold the Sea, I cannot be a worthy servant of God Vishnu."

God Vishnu hearing about Garuda's anger at the Sea, decided to talk to him in person and came to Garuda himself. As the saying goes *"Always praise a servant displaying worth, loyalty, and nobility."*

When God Vishnu arrived at his servant's house, Garuda explained "The Sea, in his pride as your servant, took the chicks of my servant and brought shame on me. I have done nothing yet because I do not want anything to dim your glory." "Well done" said God Vishnu. Let us recover the chicks from the Sea, satisfy the birds, and go on to do business in the divine city. *They also say that a master who does not punish a wrong-doing servant earns punishment for himself."*

God Vishnu took aim with his fire-arrow at the Sea and said "Villain! Return the Sand-Piper chicks or else I will reduce you to dry land." Hearing this, the Sea took fright and restored the chicks to the Sand-Pipers. Clearly, he had not assessed the strength of the birds and that of their true friends before picking a fight with them.

After Lively was persuaded to put off a fight, he asked Crafty "How does King Rusty fight? What is his technique?" Crafty replied "Usually, he lies completely relaxed on a flat rock. If his tail is drawn in, his paws tight, his ears perked up, and he watches you closely even when you are far away, he is really ready to pounce."

Then Crafty returned to Cautious who asked "So, What have you achieved?" Crafty replied "I have set them at odds against each other. Now, I must look out for my own interests and do it in secret just like the jackal called Clever did." "How was that?" asked Cautious, and Crafty told this story.

Jackal Who Tricked the Lion

There was a lion named Big Roar who lived in a dark forest with his three hangers-on: Fierce, the wolf, Clever, the jackal, and Hump, the camel. One day, Big Roar got into a fight with an angry elephant and was badly hurt. He had to go into hiding to lick his wounds while he healed. Seven days went by and he grew thin and very hungry. So he said to his starving retinue "Go find a food-animal and even in my present condition I will help you kill and carve it for food for all of us." They went far and wide but could not find any. Clever began to plot "If Hump were killed, we would have food for many days. But, since Big Roar considers him a friend, he will not kill him. So I will have to trick him into doing so. After all, you can outwit anyone if you are smart."

Clever went to Hump. "I have a tip for you which could prolong Big Roar's life and be good for you." "Tell me, please, and I will do it" said Hump. "Give up your body at 100 percent, so you can have a double body in heaven and master can live a long life on earth." "OK" said Hump "but Big Roar must call on the Death-God to guarantee the deal." Big Roar was touched by Hump's offer of sacrifice and accepted it. Hump was killed by Big Roar and torn apart by Fierce and Clever.

Then Clever got to thinking now I must get all the food just for myself. Noticing that Big Roar was covered with Hump's blood, he told him to go to the river to wash up while he and Fierce guarded the food. So the lion went to the river. When the lion was gone, Clever said to Fierce "You are starving. Why don't you go ahead and eat. I will make your apologies when Big Roar returns." So Fierce began to eat. But then Clever shouted "Drop it. The Master is coming." When Big Roar returned he saw that the heart had been eaten and he lost his temper. "Who turned our dinner into leavings! I will kill him." Fierce looked to Clever for help but Clever said "Don't look at me. You ate the heart." At which point Fierce fled for his life.

Meanwhile, there came a caravan of camels, heavily laden, that was taking a short-cut through the forest. The caravan camels all had bells around their necks to warn people and animals to keep out of the way. When Big Roar heard the bells, he asked Clever to find out what the noise was. Clever pretended to go look and came back right away, saying "Run, Master, run. The Death-God is coming. He is mad because you brought untimely death to his camel and called upon him to be guarantor." So the lion also fled in fear of his life and Clever lived on the camel meat for a long time.

*

While Crafty was gone, Lively brooded upon his best course. I cannot run without being caught. So I should go ahead and approach Rusty, the Lion King. After all, he might see me as a lowly subject and spare my life. So he started slowly and was very troubled when he saw Rusty in the fearsome posture Crafty had forewarned him about. He sank to his knees. As they say, *the timid servant never learns when the master's purpose may change.*

Meanwhile, Rusty seeing the bull in the fighting readiness position Crafty had foretold, suddenly sprang at him. Lively, though badly injured by Rusty's sharp claws, gored the lion with his horns, stepped back and stood ready to do it again.

At this point, Cautious, seeing that both were ready to kill each other, scolded Crafty. "You stupid fool! You have done a wicked deed and made enemies of friends. You have brought trouble on the whole forest just proving that you have no idea of true governance.

One needs to always first try peaceful means, and conciliation before conflict. Power without intelligence simply hastens ruin. Statesmanship includes five things: proper beginning; good resources, human and material; choice of time and place; preparedness for bad luck; and successful completion.
But our master, King Rusty, is also at fault for trusting a false friend and counselor like you and is paying a heavy price for doing so. He is ignorant of ways and methods of good rulers. Remember the counselor who got his wish? He won the king's favor and set fire to an enemy, the naked monk." "How did that happen?" asked Crafty, and Cautious explained.

Monk Who Left His Body Behind

There was a famous King, named Gold Throne, who dwelt in a big city. He was the overlord of small forest fiefdoms surrounding the city. One day a forest ranger came to him with the report that there was trouble brewing and the main trouble maker was Chief Poker. He needed to be controlled. So King Gold Throne called on his trusted minister, Counselor Sage, to take care of the problem.

When the counselor left on his errand, a naked monk arrived in the city. His name was Bare Back. He boasted of his astrological abilities and soon won over all the city residents as if he had bought and paid for each one!

The King became curious about the naked monk and his influence upon his people. So he asked Bare Back to come to the palace. The naked monk, however, postponed his visit until the next day and when he arrived, he told the King: "Sorry, your majesty, I was held up but I had to leave my body behind last night and go to heaven where the Gods asked after you." The King was so flattered that he stopped paying any attention to ruling or the ruled.

Counselor Sage returned and heard the King singing the praises of the naked monk. Invited by the naked monk to see things for himself, Counselor Sage saw Bare Back go into his cabin and he saw him lock the door from the inside. "How soon will the naked monk return?" asked the Counselor and the King explained that the naked monk left his earthly body behind in the cabin at night and returned with another, a heavenly, body, the next morning. "If that is so" said Counselor Sage "go bring a cord of wood and burn down the cabin so that when the naked monk returns he will be able to attend the King in his heavenly body." "Why do you want this?" asked the King and the Counselor asked him "Have you ever heard the story of the girl who married a snake?"

Girl Who Married A Snake

There was a Brahmin named Righteous who was very sad because his wife did not have any children which made her very unhappy. He prayed and sacrificed on her behalf until God said to him "You will have the best son in the world: handsome, good, and charming." In time, the Brahmin's wife gave birth to a snake. Other people were horrified but she loved her son and raised him with much care.

One day, the snake's mother attended the wedding of a neighbor's son. She became sad and asked her husband Righteous to find a bride for her son. "But who will give his daughter in marriage to a snake?" Still, seeing his wife so unhappy, the Brahmin decided to go in search far and wide.

On his travels, he stopped at the house of a relative where he was made welcome. On his departure the next morning the host asked the Brahmin "What are you searching for on your travels? Where will you go next?" On learning that Righteous was looking for a suitable bride for his son, the host immediately offered his own daughter.

When Righteous returned home with a beautiful young girl who was now engaged to his son, and her attendants, the people were shocked. Her own family members, when they learned the facts, were also made unhappy. But the girl said "There are only three things in this world that once given, cannot be withdrawn: the word of kings, the blessing of saints, and a girl given in marriage. Remember the poor parrot. *What will be, will be.*" "How was that?" asked the people, and the girl told this story.

Parrot Named Brilliant

The God of Immortals, Indra, once owned a very intelligent and brightly colored parrot called Brilliant. One day he was sitting on the hand of his Master when he caught a glimpse of the God of Death and backed away. The immortals surrounding God Indra were surprised and asked the parrot "Why did you back away?" "He brings harm to all living things." So they asked the Death-God to not kill the parrot as a favor to them. But the Death-God replied "It is Time who decides such things." So the immortals took the parrot with them and went to visit Time and requested the same favor. "It is Death who decides. Go see him." But when they did so, the parrot died at the mere sight of Death. Horrified, the immortals asked "What is this? What happened here?" To which the Death-God replied "Fate had simply arranged that when the parrot saw Death, he would die. It was pre-ordained."

*

Having told the story, the young bride-to-be married the Snake. One night, after some time had passed, she felt a man enter her bed. She was terrified and about to flee when the man said to her "I am your husband and have left the snake's body in my chest." When he had convinced her they spent a happy night together. Meanwhile, Righteous, woke unduly early and saw the snake skin lying in his son's room. "I should burn the chest and snake skin" he thought "then my son will not be able to return into a snake's body." So he did burn the chest and from then on the Brahmin and his wife's son was always seen in a handsome man's body with a beautiful wife beside him.

After Counselor Sage had explained his reasons for wanting to burn the cabin, the King set fire to the cabin with the naked monk's body inside.

Cautious continued to scold Crafty "The imposter, the naked monk, got his just deserts and you will too. Good advice is wasted upon a villain like you. As the saying goes you cannot teach an un-teachable monkey." "What do you mean?" asked Crafty, and Cautious told this story.

Un-Teachable Monkey

A troop of monkeys were looking to stay warm on a chilly winter evening. They found a firefly and thinking it was a spark of fire, they gathered it up carefully and put it in the middle of a bed of dry grass and leaves, and began to blow upon it. A particular Monkey blew repeatedly and with vigor on the poor firefly.

Seeing him work on his useless task, a bird named Helper, whose days were numbered, flew down from her tree and advised the Monkey to stop blowing. "This is not fire" she told him, "This is a firefly." But the Monkey paid no attention. Helper, though, kept interfering and tried again and again to make the Monkey stop what he was doing. Finally, the Monkey exploded with rage and when she next came close, he seized her, smashed her head on a rock, and killed her.

"*Advice and education are wasted on those too stupid to learn*" continued Cautious. "*Wisdom, not beauty, and an intelligent mind is rare indeed.* Remember the son who tried to be smart and suffocated his father?" "How was that?" asked Crafty, and Cautious told this story.

Honest and Sly

There were two young men, named Honest and Sly, who were good friends, both sons of merchants. When it came time to leave home, they decided to travel together to go seek their fortune in nearby cities. One day, not long after they began their journey, Honest tripped over a pot which contained a thousand gold coins and appeared to have no owner. Honest, talking it over with Sly, decided to return home for he had found his fortune after all. Sly decided to return also. When they got close to home, Honest generously offered to split his find and give half the money to his friend Sly so that they both would be welcomed back as equally successful young men.

Sly suggested they take only a hundred gold coins each with them and bury the rest as a bond to their friendship. They would always be friends because they kept their money in common. Not realizing Sly's hidden duplicity, Honest agreed.

Before long, Sly who was a real spendthrift, ran out of money and requested a second installment of another hundred dollars. Honest did not object. Within a few months, Sly had spent that money also on unwise things. Finally, he gave in to temptation and began to plan on stealing the rest of the six hundred coins. Eventually, he took all the money and covered his tracks well in the woods where they had buried the treasure.

It was not long before Sly had spent all, every penny, of the whole fortune, gambling it away on useless things and false friends. So he came up with yet another scheme. He went to Honest and suggested it was now time to divide up the money. Honest agreed but when they went to the spot where they had buried the pot, there was, of course, no money left. Sly began to loudly accuse Honest of stealing it. Honest became angry and suggested they carry their quarrel to court.

The judge looked for evidence or a witness to help him decide the case. At which point Sly said he had the Goddess of the Woods herself as a witness. So the judge ordered that the court would convene the next day in the wood.

Meanwhile, Sly rushed to get help from his father. He asked his father to hide in the hollow of a tree, pretend to be the Goddess of the Wood and bear false witness on his son's behalf. The father was very upset and replied "O Son, you *have not really thought through the consequences, sometimes the cure is worse than the disease.* Remember the stupid herons?" "What stupid herons?" asked Sly, and his father told this story.

The Cure Was Worse Than the Disease

In a big fig tree in a deep dark forest near a big lake lived a pair of Herons. Whenever the Heron-Hen laid her eggs in their nest, a long black snake that lived in a hollow in the same tree, would climb up and eat the chicks before they had grown wings. The Herons were devastated. One day, the mother Heron went to sit by the edge of the lake and could not stop crying.

A Crab noticed her and asked what was wrong. The mother Heron explained. "Can you help?" asked the Heron. But she asked the wrong creature. Herons are natural enemies of crabs, so seeing an opportunity for gain, the Crab told her to put down a trail of partly eaten fish from where the Mongoose lived in the forest to the hollow where the Snake lived. Then, he told her, the Mongoose would eat the Snake. So the mother Heron did what the Crab had advised but the Mongoose not only ate the Snake at the bottom of the fig tree but also the Herons up in the nest.

*

Sly however chose to ignore the warning of the story his father had told. Following his own plan, he helped his father hide in the hollow of the tree where the pot of money had been buried in the woods. When the Judge and court officers arrived the next day, they heard a voice in the tree bear witness against Honest. But, before the Judge could convict him, Honest had set a fire around the base of the tree, which in turn had suffocated Sly's father. Everyone realized that Sly had arranged a false witness. Where upon the Judge convicted Sly, sent him to prison, and recommended Honest for a good job in the city government.

After telling Crafty the story, Cautious continued chiding him. "You have shamed your family by destroying Lively who trusted you and in the end you are destroying our Master too. I should beware. As the saying says where the mice eat the balance-beam, the hawk can lift an elephant, let alone a boy." "What are you talking about?" asked Crafty, and Cautious told this story.

Mice That Ate Iron

There was a merchant, named Prosper, who lost all his money. So he decided to leave town and go seek his fortune elsewhere. But before he left, he pawned a valuable iron balance-beam which he had inherited and which weighed a thousand pounds.

After quite a long time, Prosper returned home and went to the Pawn-Broker to reclaim his deposit, the iron balance-beam. "I am afraid your balance-beam has been eaten by mice" said the Pawn-Broker. "Oh well" said Prosper, "Not to worry. Nothing lasts forever. Such is life. I had better go have a bath in the river now. Would you do me a favor and send your boy with me to carry my stuff?" Feeling guilty at his own trickery, the Pawn-Broker sent his son to carry the merchant's luggage for him.

After his bath in the river, prosper tied up the Pawn-Broker's son and forced him into the hollow of a tree. Then he went to the pawn-broker's shop and told him "I am so sorry but a hawk carried off your son from the river bank while I was having my bath." "How can that be? That is impossible. You are lying" shouted the Pawn-Broker in a rage. "How could mice eat my iron balance-beam?" said the merchant. "Return my balance-beam and I will return your boy." They kept arguing and went to a nearby magistrate with their quarrel. When each told his absurd story, the magistrate laughed and ordered that each return what he had wrongly taken so the merchant Prosper got his iron balance-beam and the Pawn-Broker got his boy back.

After telling the story, Cautious continued to berate Crafty. "You are a knave. You could not bear Rusty's friendship with Lively. You have succeeded in destroying what you coveted. You wanted all Rusty's favor for yourself. I don't know why I stay with you. A disaster could happen from merely associating with you. As the saying goes, *even brothers can become prime examples of good and bad education.*" "What do you mean?" asked Crafty, and Cautious told this story.

KILL HIM!   WELCOME!

Twin Parrots, Good and Bad

A Parrot couple who lived in the woods had twins but before they could raise the chicks, the parents died. As it happened, one baby chick was found by a Poacher and raised by him. The Poacher taught the Parrot to use bad and threatening words. The other twin Parrot chick was found by a wandering hermit and raised by him. The Hermit taught the Parrot chick to mimic words of welcome and praise. Time passed and the Twin Parrots came to reflect their education, bad and good.

One day, a King was riding alone in the woods. He had gotten separated from his attendants. He came unexpectedly upon the Poacher's hut. As he approached, the Parrot started squawking "Quick. Set a trap. Tie him up. Kill him." Hearing such threats, the King turned around and quickly rode off in another direction.

Later in the afternoon, the King reached the Hermit's hut. As he slowly, slowly, came near it, he heard another Parrot squawking. "Welcome, welcome. Have some food. Have some cool water. Pray with us." Upon getting such a different reception, the King began to brood upon the *differing results of associating with bad and good people.*

Having told the story, Cautious was still full of reproach of Crafty. "Just staying with you is an evil. As they say, it is better to cling to wise foes than foolish friends. Remember the robber who died for his victims and the monkey that killed the King?" "Remind me" said Crafty, and Cautious told the following two stories.

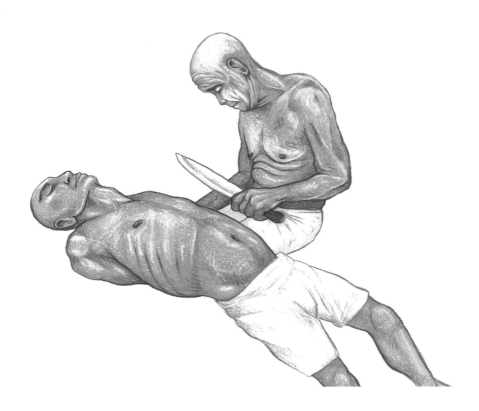

74

Sensible Foe

Once, a prince made friends with the son of a Merchant and the son of a Professor. They soon became inseparable and spent time in all sorts of pleasurable pursuits. However, the prince did not like riding horses or elephants and did not care for archery. His father, the King, decided to give him a talking-to because the Prince never engaged in the royal activities. When the prince later told his friends about the chiding that had made him unhappy, his friends said "Our fathers too keep rebuking us because we are not interested in their professions. We were enjoying our friendship and trying to ignore our problem. We see you are unhappy at home just as we are. What do you think we should do?" The prince replied " It is unmanly to stay where we are constantly chastised. Let us leave home." Having decided on what to do, the three friends considered how to proceed. "Our wishes cannot be fulfilled without money" said the Merchant's son. "So let us go to Mineral King Mountain where we may find precious stones and make our fortunes." So the three friends began their journey. There, as good luck would have it, they found a trove of priceless gems in brilliant colors. "How can we guard our treasure through the forest on our way home?" they asked themselves. The Professor's son suggested that the best plan might be to swallow the gems and carry them in their stomachs. No one would even suspect them of having anything valuable with them.

So, at dinner before setting off, they swallowed the gems. But someone had been watching them during the whole time. He thought, I too have been climbing Mineral King Mountain for many days searching for gems but without any luck. Why should the three friends get rich and not me? I will travel with these three and at nightfall, when they are asleep, I will cut open their stomach's and get the gems for myself.

So he approached the three friends and asked "Would it be all right if I join you? I don't want to be travelling alone through the dense forest below." The friends agreed and the four travelers proceeded on their journey. Near the trail through the forest was a gypsy village. It wasn't a big village but it had an Old Gypsy who kept birds that were able to foresee things most people could not. As the four travelers were passing nearby, one of the Old Gypsy's favorite birds started singing. The Old Gypsy understood most birdsong and translated for the village chief. "Those travelers have precious gems." So the Chief asked the village strongmen to catch the travelers and search them.

When they did not find anything the Chief himself frisked them and finding nothing, he let them go but kept most of their clothes. But the bird kept singing the same song, so the village Chief had them brought back and searched them one more time. Finding nothing the Chief was again about to let the three travelers go free, when the old bird sang the same song, but this time loudly, and in great anger. Since the bird had in the past always been correct in his prediction, the village Chief did not want to offend him, the Old Gypsy or others who respected it. He also began to suspect that the travelers may have swallowed the gems. So he announced that he would kill all four travelers the next morning to see if the gems were in their stomachs and tied them down for the night in the cabin that served as a prison. The three friends were silent. The captive fourth man, the thief realized that he was a dead man. When the Chief found the gems in the stomachs of the other three, he would certainly cut him open also. He remembered the proverb that when all is lost, the noble person tries to serve others even at his own expense. So he decided to offer to be the first the village Chief cut open. By making the sacrifice, he would lose his life but might save the life and wealth of the three friends and in so doing win himself glory in the life hereafter. The next morning the village chief cut open the stomach of the thief and finding nothing let the three friends go free.

Eventually, the prince inherited the kingdom and became King. He made his friend, the Merchant's son, the treasurer, and his other friend, the Professor's son, his Prime Minister. After delegating most of the onerous tasks of governing, the new King began a life of ease and luxury. He acquired a pet monkey of whom he grew unduly fond. More than fond really, he grew to have great confidence in him and even made the Monkey his personal sword-bearer.

Foolish Friend

One day, the King decided to have an afternoon nap in the classical pagoda which was beautifully located in his ornamental gardens. As he lay down, he said to the Monkey "I shall rest here in this arbor. You keep careful watch and make sure no one disturbs me." He went to sleep and the Monkey stood guard. Soon thereafter, a honey-bee arrived drawn by the nectar in the blooming flowers and hovered around. Then he alighted on the King's hair. The monkey tried to wave the bee away but the bee continued his hovering and occasional sitting on the King's curls. The Monkey got mad at the bee, drew the King's sword and swung it at the bee, a blow that cut the King's head in two.

*

"So *one should beware of making friends with fools and trusting in them too much*" continued Cautious. *"It is always best to do the right thing. You have done wrong, thinking it is in your best interest.* Just you look at what is happening now" and he pointed towards the fight before them. Rusty and Lively, each enraged at the other, had renewed the battle. The Lion, of course, won although Lively put up a good fight. But, having killed Lively, Rusty was filled with remorse. "I too have done wrong. The bull was my close friend, by killing him I have only hurt myself."

Crafty was however immediately at Rusty's side ready to flatter and give false advice. "A King is not like the common people. What is wrong in the common man can be a virtue in a king." Cautious made one last effort to reach Rusty: *"A King should consult more than one counselor and only then make up his mind before taking drastic action."* But Crafty made sure that Cautious' words were not heard.

ACKNOWLEDGEMENTS

As I have noted elsewhere, the *Panchatantra* stories (literally Five Books) have been part of India's oral and scholarly tradition for at least two thousand years or more. They have been told and retold all over the world and have influenced many literary genres, particularly those containing animal characters and 'nesting stories' i.e. one story in another story in another story. Sometime towards the end of the twelfth century, the seminal version of the *Panchatantra* was written by Vishnusharma in Sanskrit and has formed the best known rendition ever since. It is comprised of a vast array of folk wisdom interspersed with eighty-five stories which collectively serve as a guide book of sorts on how to live a wise and good life. Many translations of the text are available in English and some selected stories have been published for young children. However, the entire collection has never been adapted for casual readers, whether teenagers or adults.

My goal is to make the core of the *Panchatantra* easily accessible to the English speaking world. I have delved deeply into three authoritative, literal, translations of the complete text of the *Panchatantra* from the original Sanskrit by three eminent scholars: Arthur W. Rider (1925), Chandra Rajan (1993) and Patrick Olivelle (1997). Their work represents the best of what serious academics have to offer. I am clearly indebted to them. Nevertheless, the original in its entirety remains rather difficult to register and enjoy for non-academics. I have used their translations to understand and stay as close to the original of the *Panchatantra* as possible. Beyond that, the way I have organized the five books for a lay audience, the telling of the stories, the language used, and the summary of the wisdom highlighted by the stories, are entirely mine.

I have read and re-read the stories in various forms over the last fifty years. I wish I had a way of publicly thanking all the authors I have read on the subject of the Panchatantra. Suffice it to say, their work taught me that these ancient stories are the essence of Indian wisdom and values that deserve a wide international audience.

Throughout this venture, my husband Michael has been my strongest backer, my sharpest critic, my meticulous editor, and my most longsuffering love. I cannot thank him enough. I also owe thanks to my children, Kieran and Sean, who never failed to point out that my stories were not PC enough for children, and to my friends, Roland, Judy and Jon, who did not hesitate to point out that my story-telling was too confusing even for adults. I hope they will see that I took their judgments seriously.

I hope that my enthusiasm for these stories is catching. Cheers.

Narindar Uberoi Kelly, June 2014

MORE TALL TALES OF OLD INDIA

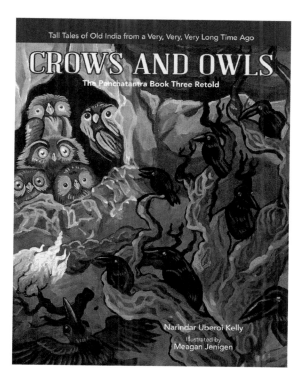

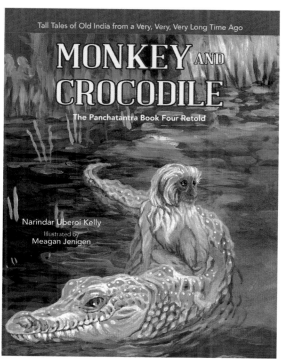

The Panchatantra Retold
Narindar Uberoi Kelly
Illustrated by Meagan Jenigen

CPSIA information can be obtained
at www.ICGtesting.com
Printed in the USA
BVXC01n1632210714
359734BV00001B/1

9 781490 740287